THE WONDERFUL WORLD OF WORDS

The Mess at Farmer Sam's

Dr Lubna Alsagoff
PhD (Stanford)

Farmer Sam worked hard.
She took very good
care of her farm.
She loved to groom
the horses...

...milk the cows,

...feed the pigs

...and collect the eggs the hens had laid.

But Farmer Sam did not like to do housework.
She did not like sweeping the floor...
...dusting the shelves,
...washing the dishes,
...or doing the laundry.
Farmer Sam's house was very messy!

Farmer Sam decided that she needed help.
But no one in WOW would help Farmer Sam with her housework. They knew how messy and dirty her house was!

So Farmer Sam decided she needed to build a robot!

Farmer Sam was very pleased with herself.

Robbie the Robot could do all the chores that Farmer Sam did not like to do!

He washed the dishes.

He swept the floor.

He dusted the bookshelves.

He cleaned the windows.

Soon, Farmer Sam's home was spick and span.

One day, Farmer Sam needed to go to the hardware store to buy some tools to fix the well.

Robbie, please look after the hens while I am gone.

I think the chicken feed is about to run out.

Please look up Gary's telephone number and order some more from his shop.

Farmer Sam left in a big hurry. She did not check if Robbie understood her.

Look after the hens?

Robbie walked to
the chicken coop.

He opened the door to the coop
and let all the chickens out.

Robbie looked at chickens running out of the coop
and ran after them!

After that, Robbie went to the storeroom to check the chicken feed.
Check if the chicken feed has run out.

Robbie was confused.
How can a bucket of food for the chickens run out of the storeroom?

Farmer Sam says
I should order some
more chicken feed.

Look up Gary's
phone number.
Robbie held Farmer Sam's
phone book up, and looked
at the book.
It was very
difficult work!

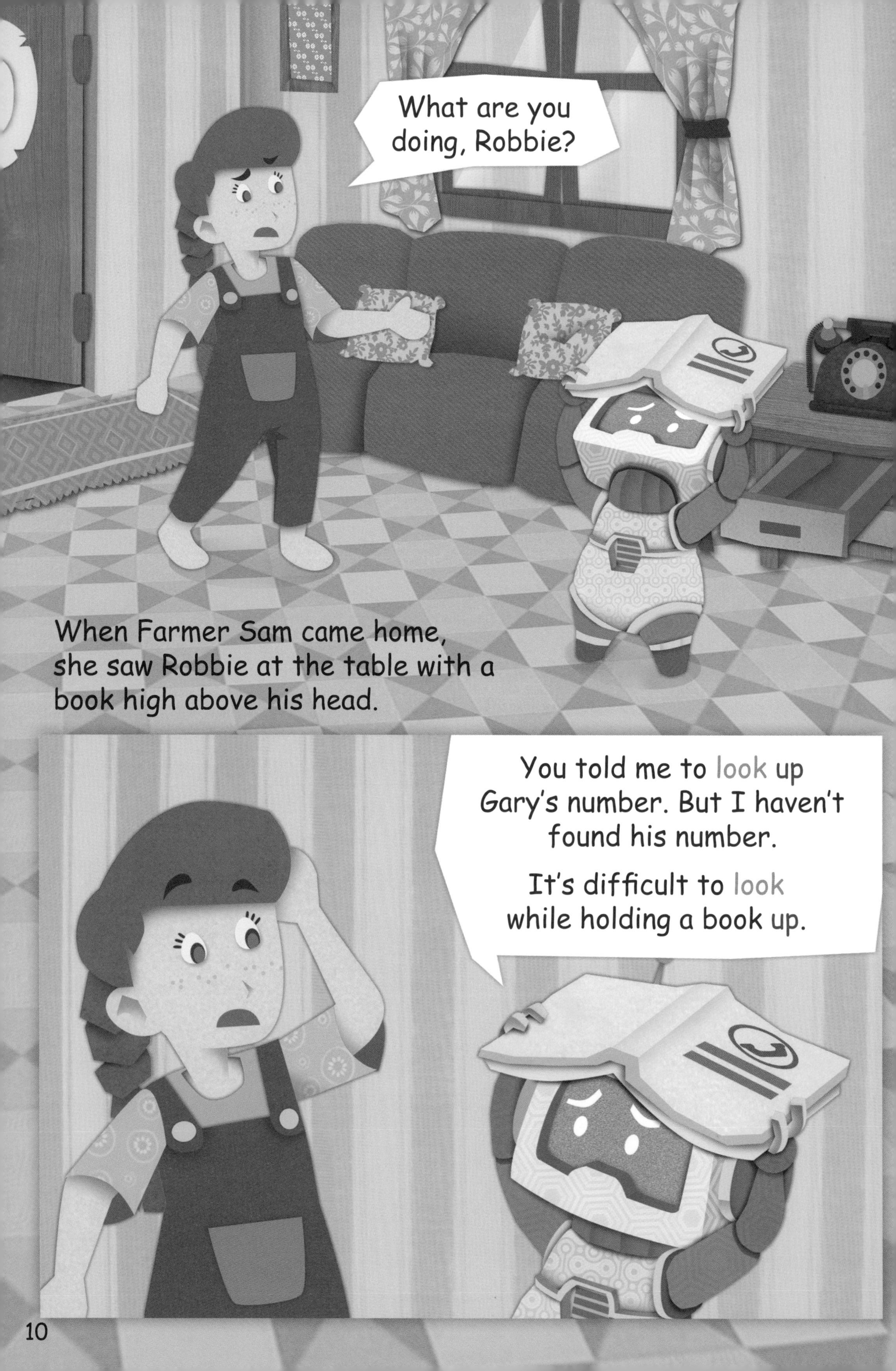
What are you doing, Robbie?
When Farmer Sam came home, she saw Robbie at the table with a book high above his head.
You told me to look up Gary's number. But I haven't found his number.
It's difficult to look while holding a book up.

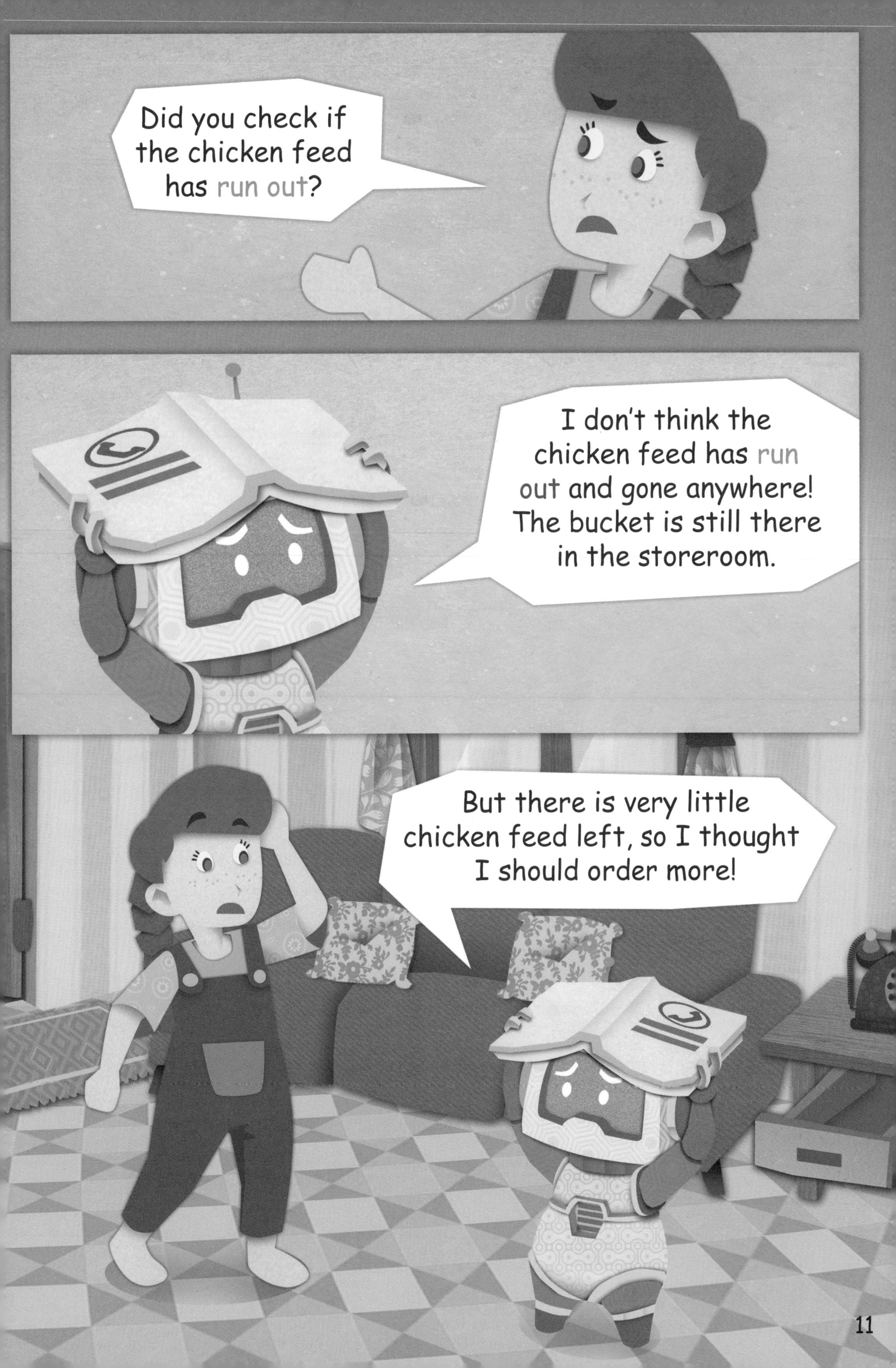
Did you check if the chicken feed has run out?
I don't think the chicken feed has run out and gone anywhere! The bucket is still there in the storeroom.
But there is very little chicken feed left, so I thought I should order more!

When she went outside, Farmer Sam was shocked to find her chickens wandering around the farm.

Robbie, why did you let the chickens out of the coop?
You told me to look after them.
The only way I could think to do that was to let them out so I could look at them and run after them!

Farmer Sam and Robbie spent many hours getting the chickens back into the coop.

Farmer Sam had to make some changes to Robbie the Robot's grammar.

Robbie could now understand phrasal verbs!

Robbie looked after Farmer Sam's chickens.

Robbie looked up phone numbers for Farmer Sam.

And Robbie checked when food had run out at the farm so he could order more!

Use the phrasal verbs to describe the pictures.

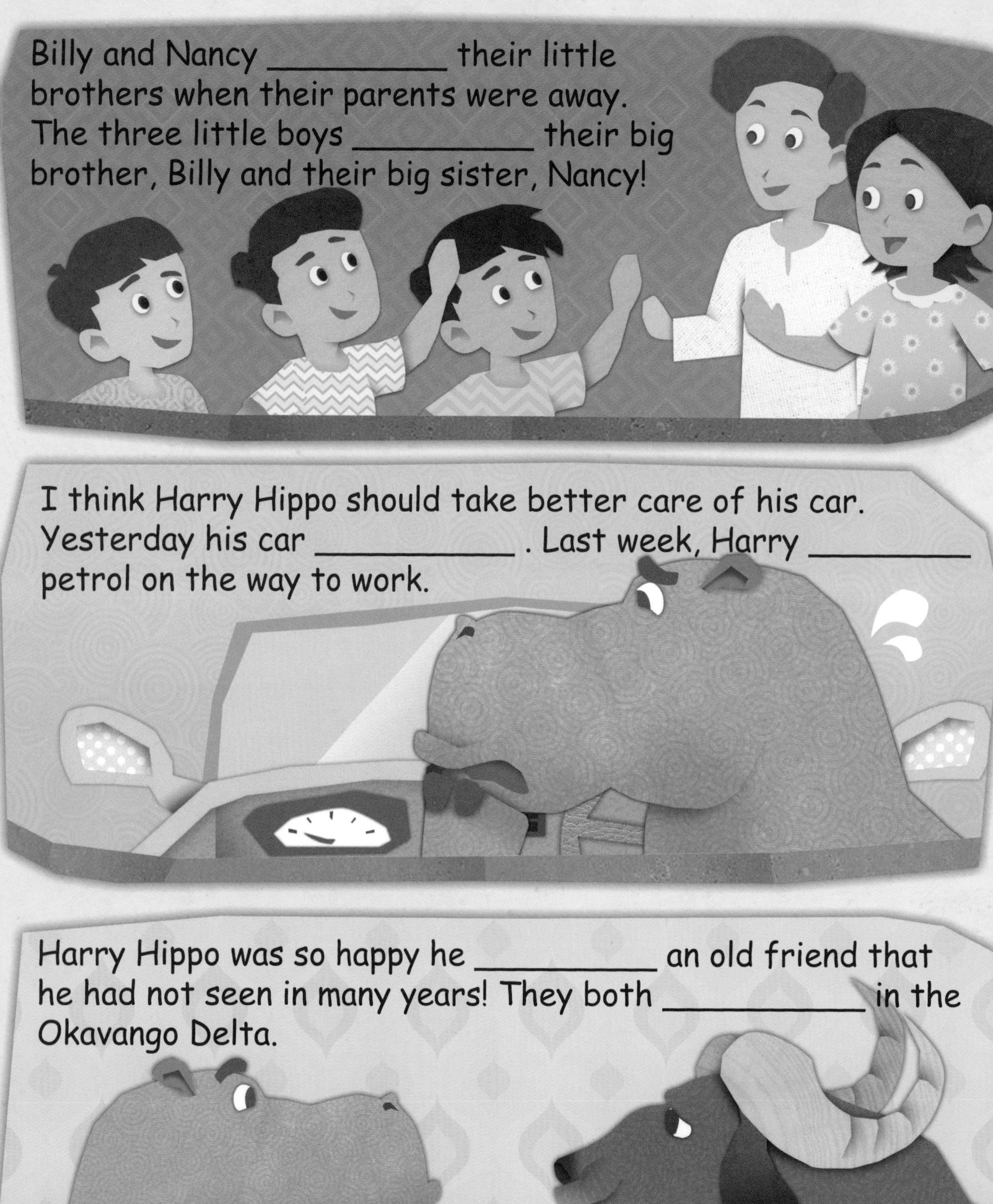

Billy and Nancy __________ their little brothers when their parents were away. The three little boys __________ their big brother, Billy and their big sister, Nancy!

I think Harry Hippo should take better care of his car. Yesterday his car ___________ . Last week, Harry __________ petrol on the way to work.

Harry Hippo was so happy he __________ an old friend that he had not seen in many years! They both ___________ in the Okavango Delta.

broke down
came up with
carried out
found out
caught up with
gave up
grew up
looked after
looked into
looked up to
ran out of
stood out
Martina ____________ as a good leader because she always ____________ many good ideas that helped her team solve difficult problems.
Constable Word ____________ the robberies and ____________ that it was a magpie that had been taking things from people's homes.
WOW
Robbie the Robot always ____________ his duties well and never ____________, even when he found them difficult.

Owl and Squirrel were sitting in the WOW School sorting the library books.
The Fabulous Forest of WOW
THE WOW GRAMMAR BOOK
GRAMMAR

I am glad that things have worked out so well with the animals.
Yes, they are all getting better.

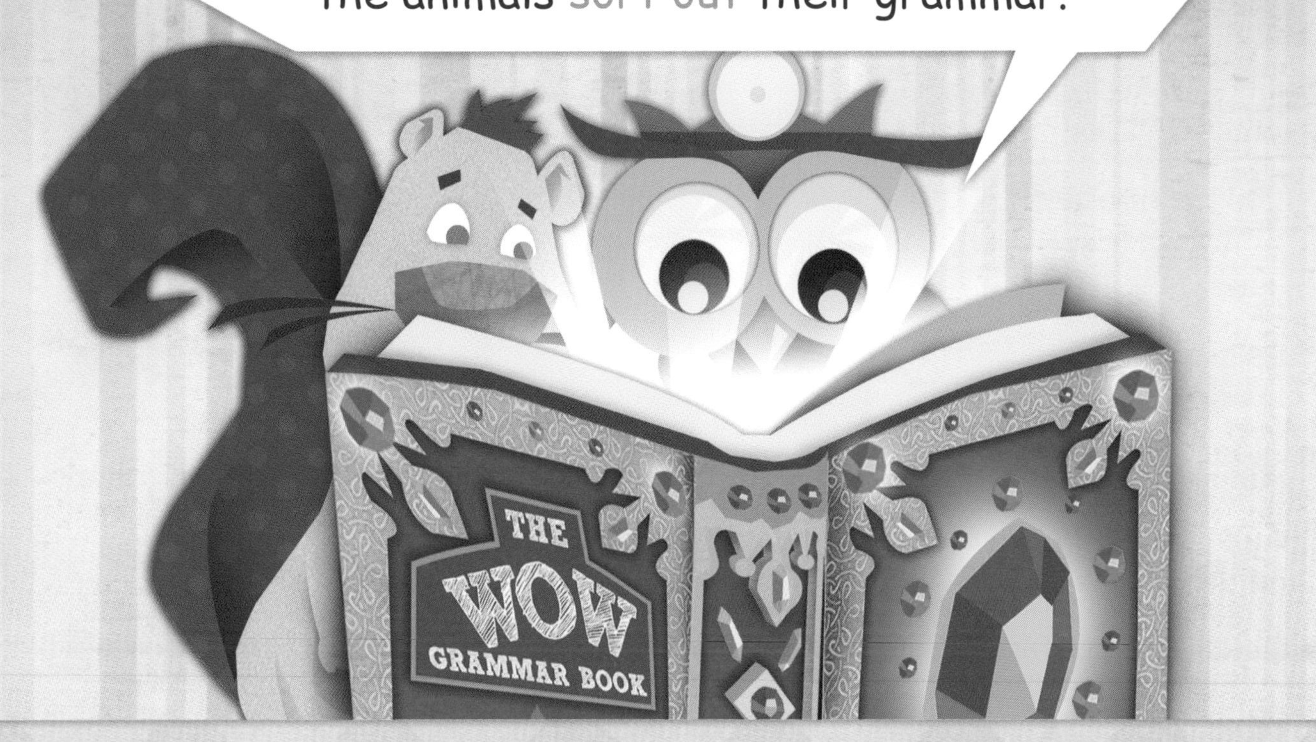

The WOW book has really helped. From it, we've been able to come up with lessons to help the animals sort out their grammar.
THE WOW GRAMMAR BOOK

Some of the animals need to catch up. They've missed quite a few lessons.

Which lessons do you think they need?

Phrasal verbs. They are so useful and some of the animals still get muddled.

Owl and Squirrel remembered what happened to Donkey when the WOW Clinic was still open.

Owl and Squirrel found Donkey sitting in the room wrapped up in bandages.

Are you alright?
I am, actually.

But you have so many bandages! You must be badly hurt.
No, I'm not.
What happened, Donkey?
Giraffe can explain!

Donkey told me that he had run into an old friend. I asked if his friend was alright.
I told her my friend was fine.

So I figured that Donkey must have been the one who was hurt!

And that was when she began to wrap me in these bandages!

Owl and Squirrel were rolling on the floor laughing.

Owl explained that Donkey used the phrasal verb run into to mean that he had met an old friend by chance.
Giraffe thought that Donkey had been running and crashed into his friend.

Use the phrasal verbs to replace the words in the sentences below.

call off | come down with | dress up | find out | get along
look out for | pass out | put off | put up with | speak up

1. Owl decided to cancel his class discussion because there was going to be a big storm.

2. Rabbit wanted to discover why his chocolate cookies kept disappearing.

3. Farmer Sam needed to postpone her appointment with the dentist to look for her lost cow.

4. Harry Hippo did not see the signs that told him to pay attention to potholes in the road.

5. Be careful not to catch the flu during the rainy season.

6. The animals could not stand Harry's bad driving habits any longer.

7. I think that penguin might faint because he is not used to the heat.

8. It would be fun to wear nice clothes for the class party!

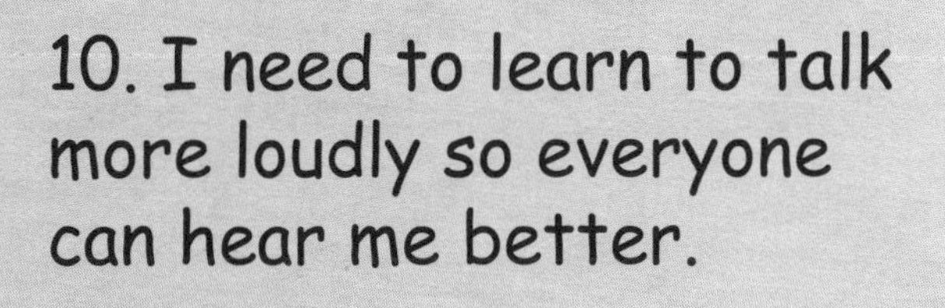

9. Neighbours should try to be friendly with one another.

10. I need to learn to talk more loudly so everyone can hear me better.

Dear Parents,

In this volume we learn about phrasal verbs. These are verbs that are made up of more than one word, but act like a single word.

A phrasal verb is made up of a verb and a particle (sometimes two). Particles are words that look like prepositions or adverbs — words like "up", "down", "away". The phrasal verb has a different meaning from the original verb and the particle(s) may also have different meanings from the prepositions or adverbs they look like. Robbie the Robot gets into trouble because he thinks that the meaning of the phrasal verb combines the meaning of the verb and the meaning of the preposition! And Donkey gets wrapped up in bandages because Giraffe thinks the same way too!

Page	Possible Answers
14	Billy and Nancy looked after their little brothers when their parents were away. The three little boys looked up to their big brother, Billy and their big sister, Nancy!
15	I think Harry Hippo should take better care of his car. Yesterday his car broke down. Last week, Harry ran out of petrol on the way to work. Harry Hippo was so happy he caught up with an old friend that he had not seen in many years! They both grew up in the Okavango Delta. Martina stood out as a good leader because she always came up with many good ideas that helped her team solve difficult problems. Constable Word looked into the robberies and found out that it was a magpie that had been taking things from people's homes. Robbie the Robot always carried out his duties well and never gave up, even when he found them difficult.
22-23.	1. Owl decided to <u>cancel</u> [call off] his class discussion because there was going to be a big storm. 2. Rabbit wanted to <u>discover</u> [find out] why his chocolate cookies kept disappearing. 3. Farmer needed to <u>postpone</u> [put off] her appointment with the dentist to look for her lost cow. 4. Harry Hippo did not see the signs that told him to <u>pay attention to</u> [look out for] potholes in the road. 5. Be careful not to <u>catch</u> [come down with] the flu during the rainy season. 6. The animals could not <u>stand</u> [put up with] Harry's bad driving habits any longer. 7. I think that Penguin might <u>faint</u> [pass out] because he is not used to the heat. 8. It would be fun to <u>wear nice clothes</u> [dress up] for the class party! 9. Neighbours should try to <u>be friendly</u> [get along] with one another. 10. I need to learn to <u>talk more loudly</u> [speak up] so everyone can hear me better.